Baby
Tugs Bear

Copyright © 1984 by American Greetings Corporation. All Rights Reserved. Published in the United States by Parker Brothers, Division of CPG Products Corp.

Care Bears, Young World of Care Bears, Tenderheart Bear, Friend Bear, Grumpy Bear, Birthday Bear, Cheer Bear, Funshine Bear, Love-a-Lot Bear, Wish Bear, Good Luck Bear, Baby Hugs Bear, and Baby Tugs Bear are trademarks of American Greetings Corporation.

Library of Congress Cataloging in Publication Data: Haas, Dorothy F. The Baby Hugs Bear and Baby Tugs Bear counting book. (Young world of Care Bears) SUMMARY: Two baby Care Bears want very much to learn to count, and as they ask the different animals in a meadow to teach them, they collect a group of one chick, two rabbits, three honeybees, etc. 1. Children's stories, America. [1.   Bears — Fiction.   2.   Animals — Fiction   3. Counting]
I.   Cooke, Tom, ill.   II.   Title.   III.   Series.
PZ7.H1124Bab   1984   [E]   84-1200   ISBN 0-910313-71-7
Manufactured in the United States of America   1 2 3 4 5 6 7 8 9 0   -01

The Care Bears

The Baby Hugs Bear and Baby Tugs Bear
Counting Book

Story by Dorothy F. Haas
Pictures by Tom Cooke

The Cloudkeeper wanted to know how many clouds, sunbeams and rainbows there were to polish in Care-a-Lot. So the Care Bears got busy counting.

Baby Hugs Bear and Baby Tugs Bear
wanted to help.

But Baby Hugs Bear and Baby Tugs Bear
could not count.

"Teach us to count, please," said Baby Tugs.

But the other Care Bears were much
too busy.

"Let's find someone who isn't busy," said
Baby Tugs Bear to Baby Hugs Bear.

"Someone who knows how to count,"
said Baby Hugs to Baby Tugs.

"Someone who will *teach* us to count,"
they said together. So they slid down
a rainbow —

and landed with a bounce in a meadow
of deep, green grass. Nearby was one
yellow chick.

"Hello," said Baby Tugs Bear. "Are you
busy? Can you count? Will you teach us?"

"I'm not busy," said the chick. "But I
can't count."

"Then we must find someone who can,"
said Baby Tugs Bear.

"May I come with you?" asked the chick.
"When you learn to count, I'll learn, too."

And the chick followed Baby Tugs and
Baby Hugs through the deep, green grass.

After a time they came to two rabbits
sitting in the sun. The rabbits were not busy.

"Hello," said Baby Hugs Bear. "Can you
count? Will you teach us?"

The rabbits twitched their noses. "We
can't count," said one.

"Then we must find someone who can,"
said Baby Hugs.

"May we come with you?" asked the
other rabbit. "If you learn to count, perhaps
we'll learn, too."

So they followed Baby Hugs and Baby
Tugs through the deep green grass.

Soon they came to three honeybees.

"Hello," said Baby Tugs Bear. "Do you know how to count? Will you teach us?"

"Buzz," said the honeybees. "We can't count because we've never learned."

"Then we must find someone who can," said Baby Tugs.

"May we come with you?" asked the honeybees. "Perhaps we'll learn to count when you do."

And they followed Baby Tugs Bear and Baby Hugs Bear through the deep, green grass, buzzing all the while.

They weren't far from a brook. There, sitting on a log, were four green frogs singing, "ba – rump, ba – rump."

"Good morning," called Baby Hugs Bear. "We want to learn to count. Can you help us?"

The frogs could croak, "ba – rump, ba – rump," but they could not count.

"We must ask someone else," said Baby Hugs.

So the Baby Care Bears continued through
the deep, green grass, and the frogs hopped
after them.

They hadn't gone far before they came to
five frolicking kittens.

"Hello," said Baby Tugs Bear. "Are you
busy? Do you know how to count? Will you
help us to learn?"

The kittens stopped frolicking. "Meow?"
they asked each other. "What is this
counting?" They all spoke at once. "Dear me
…dear us…May we come with you? We
must learn to count, too."

So the kittens followed Baby Hugs Bear
and Baby Tugs Bear through the deep,
green grass.

After a while they came to six plump geese hissing and arguing with each other. The geese looked angry.

Baby Tugs Bear wanted to act like a grown-up Care Bear so he said, "If you geese will stop arguing, you won't feel so angry. Then you can tell us how to count."

"Count?" said the geese. "Gronk, gronk. Count, you say? We don't know how to do that."

"Then we must find someone who can," said Baby Tugs. "May we come with you?" asked the geese who had now stopped arguing. "Maybe we can learn to count, too."

Then the geese, no longer looking angry, followed Baby Hugs Bear and Baby Tugs Bear through the deep, green grass.

Nearby, seven shy ladybugs were resting on a rock. The ladybugs stared at Baby Tugs and Baby Hugs and the animals who followed them.

"Hello," said Baby Tugs Bear. "Do you know how to count? Will you teach us?"

But the ladybugs were too shy to say anything.

"Oh dear," said Baby Hugs Bear. "I'm sure they don't know how to count. We must find someone who can."

But when Baby Hugs Bear and Baby Tugs Bear walked through the deep, green grass, the ladybugs followed.

It wasn't long before they came to eight
puppies taking their afternoon nap.

"Excuse me," whispered Baby Hugs.
"Will you wake up and listen?"

The puppies' eyes popped open.

"Do you know how to count?" asked
Baby Tugs. "Will you teach us?"

The sleepy puppies yawned. "What's
counting?" they asked each other. But none
of them knew.

"Then we must find someone who
knows," said Baby Tugs Bear.

"We think we'd better come with you,"
the puppies said.

"We'd like to learn to count, too."

And they followed Baby Hugs Bear and
Baby Tugs Bear through the deep, green
grass, yawning all the while.

And so they came to nine butterflies
fluttering over some flowers.

"Hello," said Baby Tugs.

"Can you count?" asked Baby Hugs.

"And will you teach us?" asked
Baby Tugs.

The butterflies fluttered and said softly,
"We would if we could, but we can't count."

"Then we must find someone who can,"
said Baby Hugs.

"May we come with you and learn to
count, too?" whispered the butterflies.

So the butterflies followed Baby Hugs
Bear and Baby Tugs Bear through the deep,
green grass.

And they came to ten turtles walking across the path very slowly.

"Hello," said Baby Hugs Bear.

"Can you count?" asked Baby Tugs Bear.

"Because if you can, we'd like you to teach us," said Baby Hugs. "Please?"

The turtles talked to each other and agreed that they couldn't count. "May we come with you?" they asked. "When you learn to count, we'll learn, too."

And the ten turtles followed Baby Hugs
Bear and Baby Tugs Bear through the deep,
green grass.

Baby Hugs and Baby Tugs were quite
tired, for they had walked a long way. They
sat down to rest in the shade of some
berry bushes.

The animals all crowded around them,
saying "Cheep, ba – rump, meow, gronk,
buzz, bow – wow — *when* will we learn
to count?"

"Oh," wailed Baby Hugs. "I *wish* all of us
could count!"

At that, there came a tinkling of bells, and
Wish Bear slid down a sunbeam. She landed
in the deep, green grass with a skip and a hop.

"When I was finished helping the Cloudkeeper, I heard you wishing to count. Counting is simple," said Wish Bear. "It just means how many of a thing there are. How many chicks are here?"

"One," said Baby Hugs.

The chick looked around and saw, sure enough, that she was the only chick there.

"How many rabbits?" asked Wish Bear.
"Two," said Baby Tugs.
All the animals looked very carefully.
They nodded their heads. Two rabbits.

"How many honeybees?" asked Wish Bear.
"Three," said Baby Tugs Bear and Baby
Hugs Bear together.
The animals could see that *three* meant
just three honeybees.

4 "How many frogs?"
"Four," said Baby Hugs. "Four, no more."
"Four," whispered the animals.

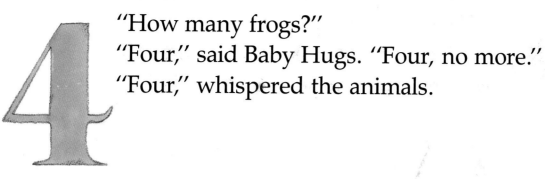

5 "How many kittens?"
"Five," said Baby Tugs. "No less."
The animals listened very carefully.

6

"How many geese?"
"Six," said Baby Hugs Bear.
"No more," said the animals, "and no less."

7

"How many ladybugs?" asked Wish Bear.
"Seven," said Baby Tugs Bear. "One more would be eight."
"One less would be six," said Baby Hugs.
"Exactly," whispered the animals.

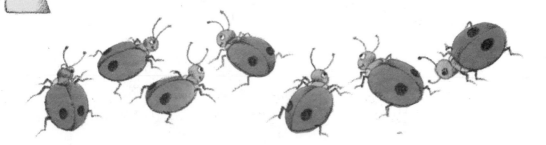

"How many puppies?"
"Eight," said Baby Hugs.
"Not seven," said Baby Tugs, "not nine — eight."

"How many butterflies?"
"Nine," said the Baby Care Bears.
"Nine," whispered all the animals.

"And how many turtles?"

"Ten," said Baby Hugs Bear and Baby Tugs Bear.

"One, two, three, four, five, six, seven, eight, nine, ten!" shouted everybody.

"No more, no less," said Baby Hugs.

"Exactly ten," said Baby Tugs.

And they were all very proud of themselves.

Wish Bear picked berries for all the
animals. There were just enough for
everyone. Exactly enough. No more, no less.

Then she took Baby Hugs Bear and Baby Tugs Bear by the paws, and they floated back to the land of Care-a-Lot.

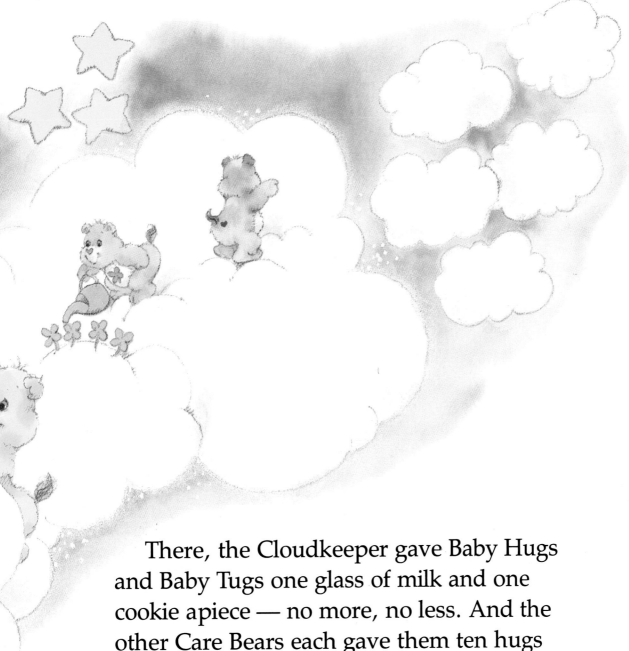

There, the Cloudkeeper gave Baby Hugs and Baby Tugs one glass of milk and one cookie apiece — no more, no less. And the other Care Bears each gave them ten hugs because they were so proud of Baby Hugs Bear and Baby Tugs Bear

WHO KNEW HOW TO COUNT!

Baby
Hugs Bear